All or Nothing

A Mexican tale retold by Julie Ellis
Illustrated by Celeste Goulding

Chapter 1

Pedro Finds the Cave

"There's gold hidden in the hills behind ***Matamoros****. Gold that was hidden by pirates a long time ago. I know it's there because my friend Reynaldo told me. His great-grandfather Pedro found it. Pedro found it, then he lost it again. This is the story that Pedro told Reynaldo and Reynaldo told me."*

When Pedro was a young man, he worked on a ranch in Mexico as a **charro** looking after cows. One day, as he was riding along behind the herd, a snake startled a cow. The cow ran off into the hills. Pedro gave chase, but the cow had disappeared.

Pedro had to find the cow. He rode far into the hills looking for it. The sun beat down on his back and, after a while, he began to feel very hot and tired.

At last he saw a cave nearby that looked cool and dark. Pedro decided to rest there. He left his horse under a tree and went into the cave.

As his eyes got used to the dark, Pedro stared in amazement. The walls of the cave were covered in drawings of fierce pirates fighting sea battles. Someone else had been in the cave before him!

Pedro walked deeper and deeper into the cave. The drawings were so real that he could almost smell the smoke from the battles, and hear the cries of the fighting men.

Then Pedro saw something even more strange than the drawings.

In the middle of the cave floor was a huge brown chest.

"What's this?" said Pedro to himself. "And what's it doing here?"

Chapter 2

Todo o Nada!

Pedro went over to the chest and tried to open it. The lid of the chest was heavy, but Pedro was strong. After much pushing, he managed to lift the lid up.

When he looked inside, he could hardly believe his eyes. The chest was full to the top with gold rings, gold coins and **pieces of eight**.

"I'm rich! I'm rich!" Pedro yelled, pushing his hands into the bright shiny gold.

Just then, a loud voice thundered at him, **"TODO O NADA!"**

Pedro looked around but he couldn't see anyone.

"TODO O NADA!" the loud voice thundered again.

Todo o nada means 'all or nothing', thought Pedro. I have to choose all or nothing. Why, that's easy! I'll take *todo* – all of the gold.

He tried to pick up the chest, but it was too heavy. Then he tried to pull it, but it wouldn't move. Pedro realised that he couldn't take the huge chest with him. Instead he started filling his pockets and his **sombrero** with gold.

When he had as much gold as he could carry, Pedro stumbled towards the front of the cave. As he did, there came a great rumbling noise. Rocks fell in front of him, covering the cave entrance. Again Pedro heard the loud voice, **"TODO O NADA!"**

Pedro thought for a minute, then he called out, "I understand. I will take *nada*." At once he emptied the gold out of his sombrero and his pockets.

"I have no gold now," he called to the voice. "Please let me out of here."

Again a great rumbling was heard. This time the rocks rolled away from the cave entrance. Quickly Pedro ran out into the sunlight, where he soon began to feel better.

"I'll come back with a bag," he thought, "and I'll take all of the gold. But I'll have to ask the other charros to help me because there is too much for me to carry."

Pedro left his sombrero on the tree to mark the entrance to the cave. Then he leapt on his horse and rode back into the hills.

Chapter 3

Pedro Tells the Charros

It was late evening when Pedro arrived at the ranch, and several charros were sitting outside talking.

"You'll never guess what happened to me today," Pedro said to them excitedly. "I found a chest full of pirate gold in a cave up in the hills."

"You've been in the hot sun too long," laughed one of the charros.

"You probably fell asleep and dreamed you found gold," said another charro.

"I did find gold! My pockets were full of it," cried Pedro, pulling his pockets inside out.

The charros fell silent. They were all staring at Pedro's pockets, which were lined with gold dust glinting in the moonlight. The charros could see that there really had been gold in Pedro's pockets, and suddenly everyone got very excited.

For many years, after that night, the hills swarmed with men looking for the cave. They never found it or the gold. And to this day, Pedro's sombrero has never been seen again.

"There's gold hidden in the hills behind Matamoros. Gold that was hidden by pirates a long time ago."